OH NO, Little Dragon!

To Ed
T. S. I. M. H.
with special thanks to
the Revisionaries

ATHENEUM BOOKS FOR YOUNG READERS • An imprint of Simon & Schuster Children's Publishing Division •
1230 Avenue of the Americas • New York, New York 10020 • Copyright © 2012 by Jim Averbeck • All rights reserved,
including the right of reproduction in whole or in part in any form. • ATHENEUM BOOKS FOR YOUNG READERS
is a registered trademark of Simon & Schuster, Inc. • For information about special discounts for bulk purchases,
please contact Simon & Schuster Special Sales at 1-866-506-1949 or business@simonandschuster.com. • The Simon &
Schuster Speakers Bureau can bring authors to your live event. For more information or to book an event,
contact the Simon & Schuster Speakers Bureau at 1-866-248-3049 or visit our website
at www.simonspeakers.com. • Book design by Ann Bobco • The text for this book is set in Adobe Caslon
Pro. • The illustrations for this book were created using handmade papers and oil pastel on textured paper,
digitally assembled and enhanced in Photoshop. • Manufactured in China • 0512 SCP • First Edition •
10 9 8 7 6 5 4 3 2 1 • CIP data for this book is available from the Library of Congress. •
ISBN 978-1-4169-9545-6 (hardcover) • ISBN 978-1-4424-4270-2 (eBook)

OH NO, Little Dragon!

atheneum books for young readers

New York London Toronto Sydney New Delhi

Little Dragon had a spark in his heart,
so he could huff and puff and . . .

PHOOSH.

PHOOOOOOOOOOOOOOOSH!

"Oh Little Dragon," Mama said, "I truly love your flame.

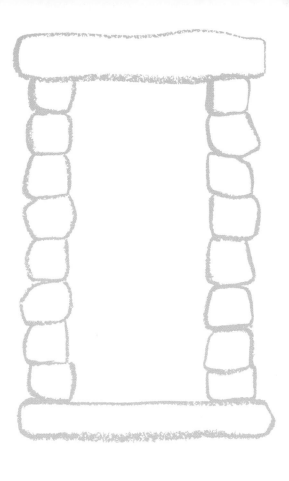

"But look how sooty you are.
Time for a bath."

OH NO!

"I hate taking baths," Little Dragon said.

"You can play with your new wooden boat," said Mama.

"Okay . . . ,"
grumbled Little Dragon.

"Grrrrrr!" Little Dragon growled.

"You are toast."

Then he huffed and puffed and . . .

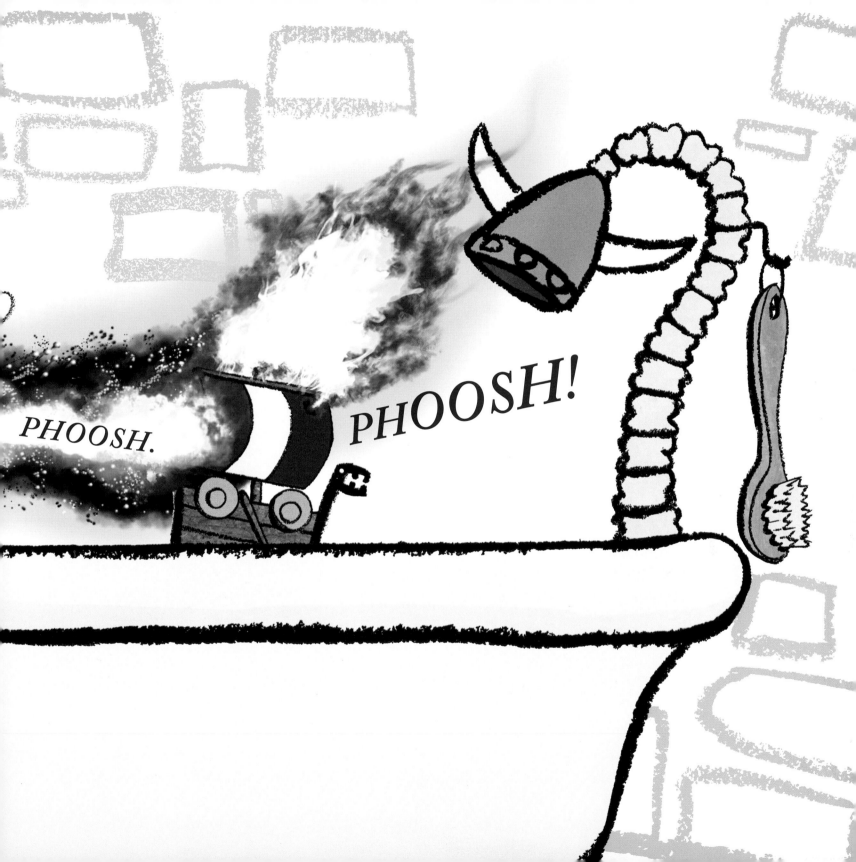

OH NO!

Little Dragon Fire Department
to the rescue.

Cannonba

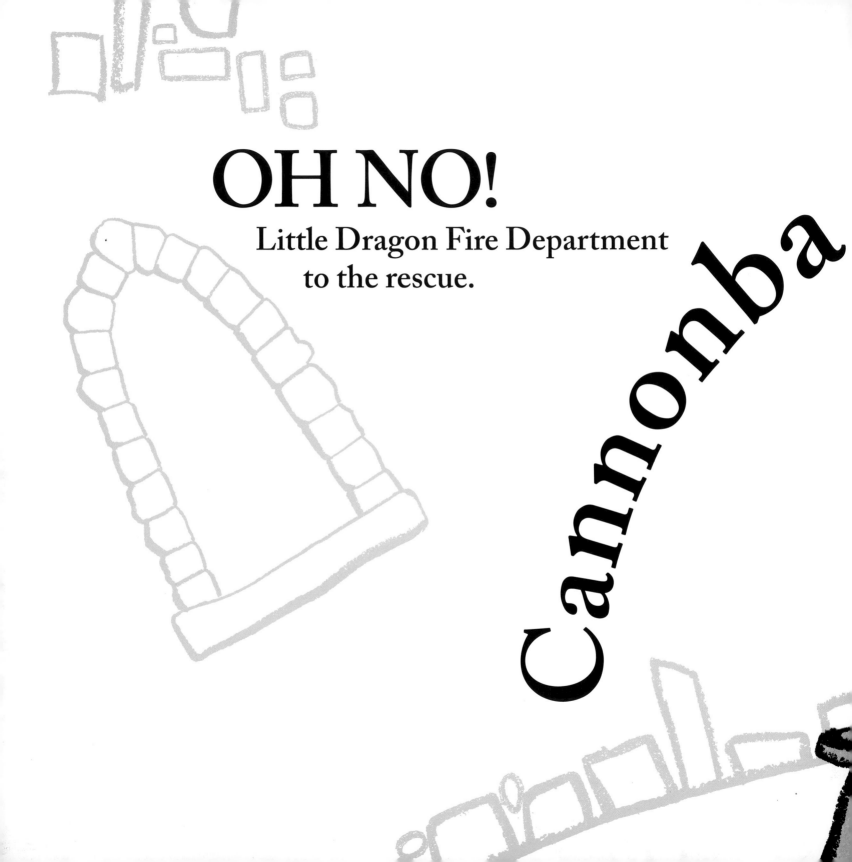

aaaaallllll!

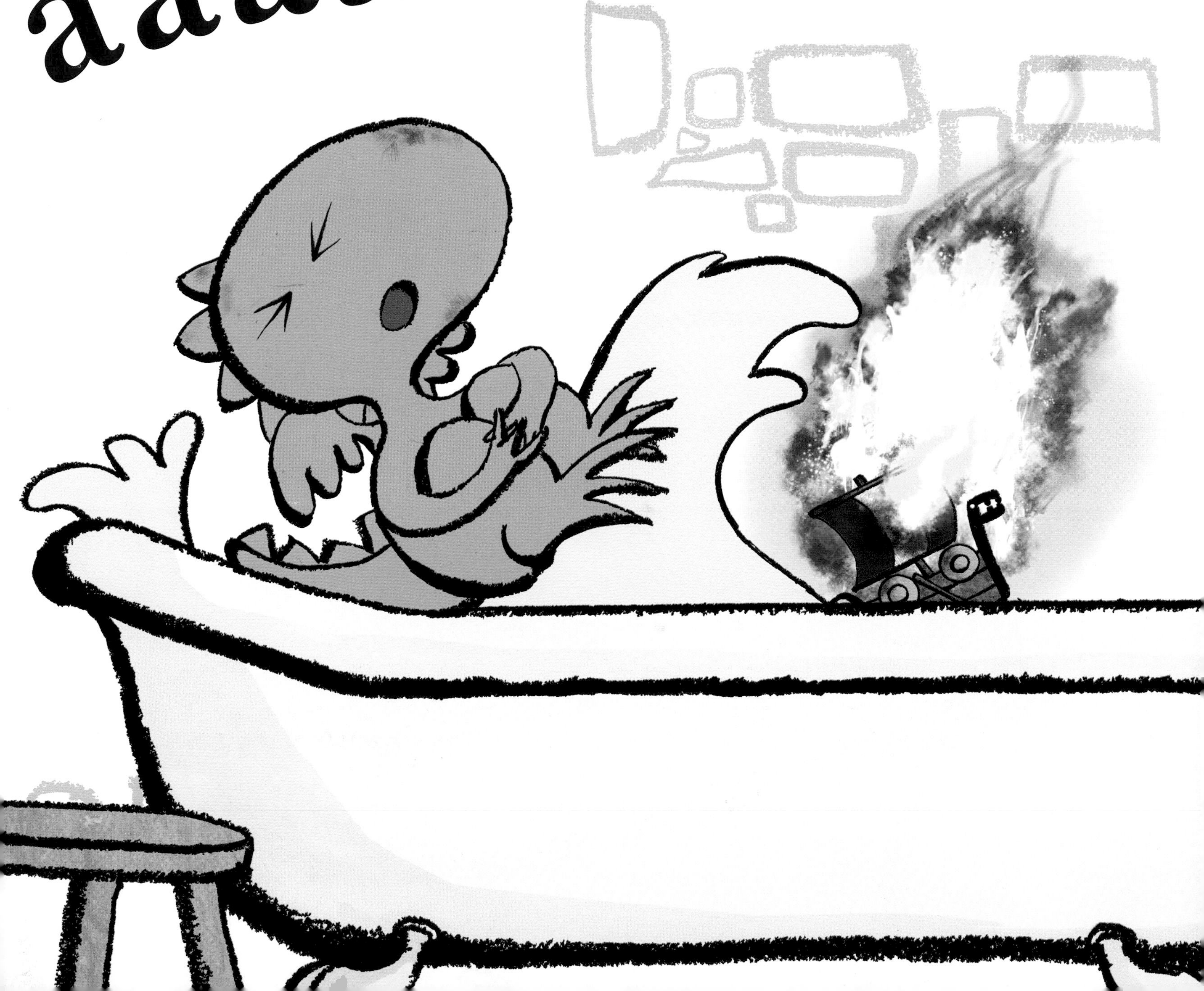

Hahahahahahaha

OH NO!

The water doused Little Dragon's spark.

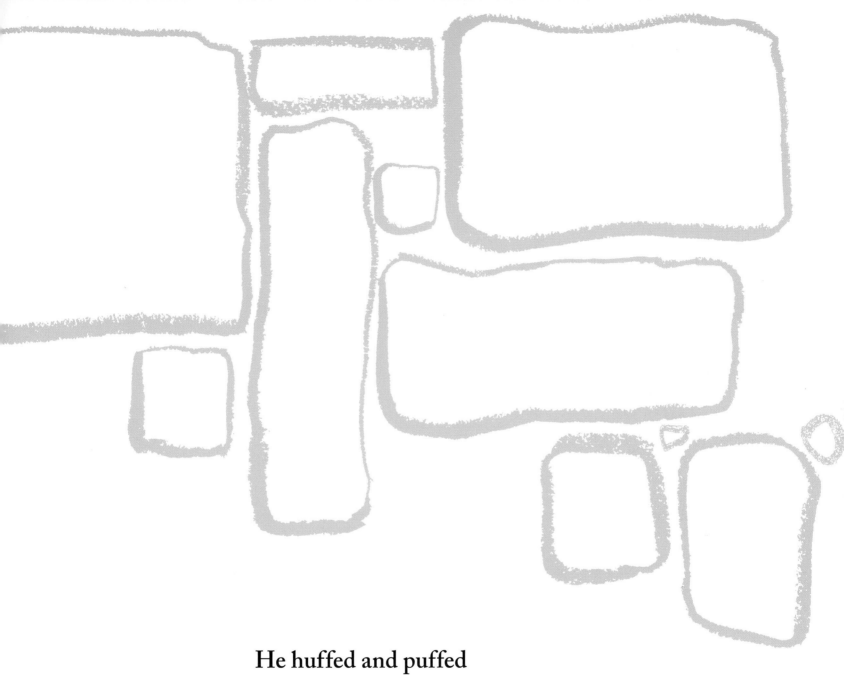

He huffed and puffed

and puffed and huffed,

but not a flicker of flame would come out.

Little Dragon thumped his heart
and rubbed his tummy
to restart the spark,
but . . .

OH NO!

That only gave him a cherry belly.

So Little Dragon bundled into every stitch of winter clothing from his closet, but . . .

OH NO!

That only made him all sweaty.

Little Dragon dashed
to the kitchen and ate the
three hottest chili peppers
from the bowl.

But . . .

OH NO!
That didn't restart the spark in his heart.

It only made his eyes water.

And they wouldn't stop.

Plink

Plunk

Plop

"Why are you crying, Little Dragon?" Mama asked.

"Because," Little Dragon said,
"if I don't have my flame,
you won't love me anymore."

"Oh no, Little Dragon," Mama said. "I could never stop loving you . . ."

"because YOU are the spark in MY heart."

Then she kissed
him on his freshly
scrubbed snout.

Little Dragon
felt warm inside.

Warm inside?

Could it be?

OH YES!

Little Dragon huffed and puffed and . . .

PHOOOOOOOOOOOOOSH!

Oh no . . .

sooty again!